A GEEKS AND THINGS COZY MYSTERY

Forgive and Forget

S.E. BIGLOW

1

An unusually oppressive early morning summer heat shimmered on the pavement as Kalina Greystone took off at a steady jog from the front of her shop, Geeks and Things. She had barely taken enough steps to get to the next block on Main Street when her phone beeped at her, displaying the temperature: 81 degrees. At seven in the morning.

"Wonderful," she groaned before settling

on a playlist and picking up the pace. Heat or no heat, she needed to get her run in before she had to open up for the day.

The end of summer was a big money maker for the shop, especially with kids getting ready for school. There was little doubt in her mind that most of the teenagers in town would be turning in summer reading lists crammed with comics and graphic novels. She only felt a little guilty that the next generation wasn't reading actual books.

The notion that this was *her* shop, *her* livelihood, had finally settled in. People in town had stopped comparing the way she ran the business to her father—at least to her face—and it made the decision to come back home to Ellesworth feel like the right call. The little seaside town moved at a slower pace to the city, where she'd spent most of her adult life, but it had some perks, too. She'd managed to reconnect and rekindle a spark with her high school sweetheart, Christian Harper.

Kalina took a sharp left and sucked in a deep breath as she took the hill leading in the direction of the cemetery and the town's one church. As her heart pounded in her ears from the exertion, she flashed back to three months ago when she and Chris had stood in the cemetery and solved a pair of murders. The frenzy surrounding Aunt Agatha and Ms. Ellicott's passing had finally died down and the town was back to being quaint and normal. Kalina's phone buzzed in her pocket and she pulled it out to see a text from Chris asking her if they were still on for dinner. She smiled and slowed to a walk before responding that they were definitely on for dinner. They were lucky that their first break-up had been amicable. They were on different life tracks and they had been mature enough to get that. When he held her hand or kissed her goodnight she still felt like a giddy schoolgirl. Of course, she'd dated in college and grad school but being with Chris now was different. They were finally in a place where they could be together as adults and make it work.

Phone stowed back in her pocket, Kalina took off at a sprint to make it up and over the hill and settle back into a comfortable pace. As she ran she spotted Theo Maxwell in his boxers and undershirt scooping up the morning paper. He blushed bright red and waved before darting back inside. She chuckled to herself and took the next right, heading past the church. The door eased open and a lone figure stepped out looking subdued and tired. Leslie Mayfair, the former almost-Mrs. Cahill. A pang of sadness tightened Kalina's chest as she watched the usually bubbly school teacher hunch her shoulders on her way to her car. She hadn't known her fiancé had been killing little old ladies for sending his innocent father to prison. They made eye contact for a brief, uncomfortable moment and Kalina opened her mouth to say

'Good morning' but held her tongue. Leslie yanked her car door open and climbed into the driver seat.

Kalina waited until the car was out of sight before continuing her morning circuit. Sweat glistened on her bare arms and matted her short, auburn curls to her forehead as she veered away from the church and out towards the coast. Only a handful of people lived out by the water these days thanks to beach erosion. The salty air was a few degrees cooler and she sucked in a big gulp. Trying to shake the unease from seeing Leslie, Kalina put on another burst of speed and took the rolling slope of Ocean Front Lane at a decent clip. Her phone vibrated again and, in her earbuds, an automated voice announced that AJ was calling.

"Answer call," she said and slowed to a walk. "Hey, AJ, what are you doing up this early?"

"Hey, Aunt K. I was just checking in. I wanted to see if you needed help at the store today," her nephew answered.

He had done a lot of 'checking in' in the last couple months. Not that she minded. It put her mind at ease that he was doing okay after watching Aunt Agatha die. "If you want to stop by this afternoon you can. I don't know that I'll have too much for you to do, though."

"Great. Are you okay?"

Kalina continued along Ocean Front at a slow pace, getting her heart rate back down to normal. "Yeah, I'm just out for a run."

"Oh. You've been doing that a lot since..."

He didn't have to finish the thought for her know what he meant. "We all cope in different ways. And I could use the exercise."

Kalina rounded a bend in the street and a three-story house came into view. It belonged to the Larrabees. She'd been friends with their daughter, Nadine, in high school. Normally it wouldn't have drawn her attention in the cookie-cutter section of town. Today, she stopped and stood with her mouth hanging open. A man's body lay prone in the middle of the house's small driveway and a woman about Kalina's age sat on the front steps, rocking back and forth.

"Aunt K., are you there?" AJ's voice sounded tinny in her earbuds.

"I have to call you back," she said and yanked the buds from her ears. She moved into view slowly so as not to startle the woman. "Nadine?"

The woman looked up and Kalina saw her eyes shine with fresh tears. At this distance she could see Nadine's hands covered in what Kalina assumed was blood. A dark stain had spread under the man's head on the asphalt. "Oh, God. What did I do?" Nadine whimpered.

Kalina pulled the cord out of the headphone jack of her phone and dialed 911. She waited for the operator to give the standard response before speaking. "I need an ambulance at 1609 Ocean Front Lane. Send the police, too. A man is dead."

2

Ignoring the operator's order to stay on the line, Kalina shoved her phone in her back pocket and slowly approached Nadine, hands held out in front of her in a placating gesture. Nadine continued to rock back and forth, her gaze glued to the dead man in the driveway. Kalina moved to the left to block the view in the hopes it would snap her old friend out of her trance. Nadine finally blinked and a tear trickled down her nose and landed precariously on her upper lip. Careful not to interfere with what might be considered the crime scene, Kalina bent down in front of her friend and placed a hand on the woman's shoulder.

"Nadine. It's Kalina Greystone. I've called the police." Her tone was barely above a whisper.

Nadine blinked again and her shoulders relaxed the slightest bit at Kalina's words. It had been a good fifteen years since they'd really seen each other and Nadine looked like she'd been through some tough times—the dead body notwithstanding. The last time they'd seen each other—a week before they both headed off to college—Nadine had been all wild curls and caramel complexion. Now her hair hung limply around her face in a tangled, stringy mess and her cheeks were sunken.

"Kal? What ... what are you doing here?" Nadine asked in a scratchy voice.

"I was on a run and I found you." Kalina

glanced over her shoulder as sirens wailed in the distance. Emergency personnel would arrive soon and she would be shunned aside so Nadine could be questioned officially. She would make good use of the limited time she had left. "Nadine, honey, what happened?"

"I... I don't know." She scrubbed at her face, smearing blood from her fingertips onto her cheeks. "I think ... maybe I did it. I can't remember." She erupted into a fresh onslaught of tears. "I'm not crazy. I swear I'm not."

Kalina made soft, shushing noises and patted her friend's shoulder. "It's okay. Everything will be fine. Just try to calm down."

The siren wails grew more insistent and Kalina did her best to comfort Nadine while getting a look at the dead man on the pavement. It had been a while but it looked like Nadine's father. She couldn't be sure, though, and she wasn't about to go rifle through a dead man's pockets to be sure. That wasn't her job.

"Damn," she groaned. She'd promised herself she wouldn't get dragged into something like this again. But Nadine had been a good friend and she needed Kalina.

Tires squealed and a familiar car pulled up to the curb. An ambulance rolled up and two paramedics jumped out of the rig. Kalina stood up and turned just as Chris let out an exasperated sigh. "Hi," she said.

"I should have known."

Kalina arched a brow and closed the gap between them. "What's that supposed to mean?"

"When people die from mysterious causes you seem to always be around."

"That was one time. And I wasn't the only person there."

He nodded and peered over her shoulder at Nadine. "Want to tell me what you're doing here with a woman covered in blood and a dead man in the driveway?"

"I was out for a run before opening up and I saw Nadine sitting there and the body. I called you guys as soon as I saw it. I didn't touch anything."

Chris pointed to the front door, which sat wide open. "That was like that when you got here?"

"Yes. And Nadine hasn't moved."

One of the paramedics tended to Nadine, checking her over for any injuries, while the other checked Mr. Larrabee. "He's been dead maybe a few hours. We'll have to get him to the morgue for a better time of death."

"Don't move. We aren't done," Chris said and turned his back, pulling his phone from his shirt pocket. He dialed and then said, "This is Detective Christian Harper, Ellesworth PD. We are going to need an ME assist and a second ambulance." He ended the call and hit what Kalina assumed was a saved number. "Jimmy, it's Chris. I need you to get to my current location to secure the scene."

Suddenly chilled, Kalina wrapped her arms around her torso and watched the paramedic help Nadine to her feet. Without the distraction of Nadine sobbing on the front steps, Kalina studied the rest of the scene. How had Mr. Larrabee ended up on the driveway? She noted an open window on the second floor. Was the fall enough to kill him? Chris hung up and pivoted back to face her. "Did Nadine say anything to you?"

Kalina shivered again. "She was pretty incoherent. I think she was mostly in shock. I mean her father's dead right in front of her."

"Detective," the medic who had been tending to Nadine called, "she doesn't have any visible signs of injury. I'd guess the blood is his."

Kalina watched as they shared a look. She didn't need to be law enforcement to interpret the slight downturn of his mouth or the way his shoulders tensed. She may not have mentioned that Nadine claimed to be guilty, but he would find out sooner or later.

"I'd like to go to the hospital with you. She might feel more comfortable opening up if I'm there," Kalina blurted.

"Fine. But you are there for moral support. Nothing else. And you're riding with me," Chris said.

"Okay."

They waited until Jimmy and the second ambulance arrived. The paramedic who climbed out of the back sported a digital camera. Apparently, they weren't waiting for the crime scene technicians from Salem to show up to take Mr. Larrabee's body for autopsy. They headed off to the hospital as the paramedic snapped a few shots and his partner laid a sheet over the corpse. Kalina buckled into the passenger seat and looked at Chris. "I guess we won't be doing dinner tonight, after all."

3

The car ride was silent as Kalina and Chris made the short journey to the hospital. Chris had the air blasting and, despite the heat outside, her arms broke in goose bumps. She tried to read his expression in the rearview mirror but he wouldn't meet her gaze.

"Chris, don't be mad at me. I swear I didn't mean to stumble on a dead man on my morning run. And I promise I'll stay out of the way."

He didn't respond at first. His hands tightened around the steering wheel and his knuckles turned pale. "I'm not mad at you, Kal. I just... After what happened with Dan Cahill I thought... I thought things would go back to normal. We don't have people getting murdered in this town."

She reached over and pressed her hand reassuringly against his shoulder. "I know."

Chris had taken Captain Cahill's vendetta harder than most. She couldn't really blame him. His mentor had fallen hard from grace. It was a tiny consolation that Chris had managed to broker a plea deal for the real culprits behind Alice Beech's murder and Samuel Gordon's false conviction. Andrew Paxton and his father would be spending the next decade behind bars. Before either of them could say anything more, her phone buzzed and the store's number flashed on the screen.

"Sorry, I need to take this," she said and

hit 'Accept'. "Hello, this is Kalina, how can I help you?"

"Aunt K., it's me," AJ said on the other end of the line. "I came by the shop but you aren't here. And you hung up earlier."

Kalina bit the inside of her lip. She'd forgotten she'd given him a key in case of emergencies. She should have expected his end-of-summer restlessness to result in an earlier-than-promised visit. "I know. Something came up. I'm not sure when I'll be back to the shop."

"I can handle things if you want."

"That's sweet, but no. You aren't old enough and you don't actually work at the shop. Just close up and lock the front door for now, okay? People can deal with waiting for their comics a little longer today."

"Okay. Oh, there's some sort of delivery scheduled for this afternoon. I checked the calendar. What should I do about that?"

Kalina opened her Calendar app and saw

she was expecting a delivery of new Valiant Comics. "Damn. I'll handle it."

"What's going on? You sounded kind of freaked out earlier."

The hospital loomed ahead of them. "I'll fill you in later. I have to go."

Chris eased into the parking lot and pulled into a spot near the doors to the emergency room without another word. Kalina shoved her phone back into her pocket and climbed out of the passenger seat. She didn't see the ambulance that had transported Nadine but she assumed it had beaten them there. Chris turned to look at her and his expression softened for a moment.

"I'll make dinner up to you," he said and kissed her cheek.

"Don't even worry about it. Just focus on your job. We have plenty of time for dinner dates."

She resisted the urge to take his hand as they walked into the hospital side by side.

True to her word, she stayed quiet as he asked the young man at the registration desk where to find Nadine. Chris finally ushered Kalina out of the waiting room and back to a small, curtained-off area. Nadine lay on a bed with an IV already hooked up at the crook of her elbow. She looked less frantic, her eyelids drooping heavily. The paramedics had at least tried to clean the blood off her hands.

"Miss Larrabee, I'm Detective Harper. I'm with the police. Do you remember meeting me at your house?"

Nadine nodded her head but didn't speak. Kalina moved to sit beside her old friend and pressed her hand gently against Nadine's blanket-covered knee. Just enough to let the woman know she wasn't alone.

"Do you mind if I ask you a few questions about what happened?"

Nadine's gaze flickered in Kalina's direction and tears glistened. Kalina gave the woman a smile. "I'll be right here. Detective Harper just wants to help."

Nadine wet her lips and sat up a little straighter. "Okay." Her voice cracked on the last syllable.

Chris retrieved a small pad and pen from his pocket and sat on a stool on the other side of the bed. Kalina felt Nadine tense up beneath the blanket. She had to fight to keep from interfering. She knew Chris was only doing his job by questioning Nadine.

"Can you tell me what happened to your father?"

"I... I found him on the driveway this morning."

"So the blood on your hands was from checking on him?"

"Y-yes."

"Can you think of anyone who might have wanted to hurt your father?"

"No. I hadn't been in his life until recently. We had a falling out after my mother..."

Kalina bit her tongue—wincing at the pain—to keep from interjecting to ask about Mrs. Larrabee. Fresh tears rolled down Nadine's cheeks as Chris simply nodded in understanding.

"So you didn't hear anything at all last night?"

"I don't remember... It's all kind of a blur. Please, I'm tired. I'd like to rest now."

On cue, a nurse clad in pale purple scrubs appeared, chart and a plastic container of pills in hand. "I'm afraid you're going to have to come back later if you have more questions. The doctor has ordered that Ms. Larrabee be sedated."

Nadine's eyes grew to the size of quarters and she tried to wiggle away from the nurse as she approached. "No. I don't want them. Get away from me!"

Chris had already moved to get out of the way of the medical staff and he grabbed Kalina by the wrist, pulling her free as more staff in scrubs flooded the tiny area. They held Nadine down until someone got the medication into her. Kalina's pulse quickened as she watched how the girl she'd known for years was manhandled into submission. There were missing puzzle pieces in all of this and she was going to find out exactly what had happened.

4

—————

With Nadine safely unconscious —at least for now—Kalina and Chris headed back to the parking lot. The day continued to heat up and Kalina wiped the sweat from her neck before slipping back into the passenger seat.

"Can you drop me at the shop?" she asked.

"Yeah, sure. I need to head back to the scene to make sure it's being processed."

"You don't trust Jimmy?"

Chris shrugged. "He's still pretty green

and I think it would make him feel better if I was there."

The engine hummed to life and silence fell between them. Kalina wanted to ask Chris what he knew about Nadine's past and her mother but she kept quiet. He would no doubt tell her to stay out of it and that this was a police matter. She still refused to believe that Nadine was capable of harming anyone, let alone her father. Chris took a sharp left onto Main Street and pulled up in front of Geeks and Things, the car still idling.

"I'll call you if I can get away later." He kissed her cheek again.

She returned the gesture, holding it a little longer than necessary. "Bye."

Kalina shivered in the heat and watched Chris pull away and disappear down the street. She fished her keys from her pocket and jammed them into the lock on the shop's front door. The sign read 'Closed' so at least AJ had done as she'd asked. She could do a little archive browsing from the comfort of the shop and be there for the new shipment before trying to find out what she could about the crime scene. She flipped the light switch by the front door and waited for the energy-efficient bulbs to brighten the storefront. Turning the sign to 'Open', Kalina headed for the small bathroom and a waiting change of clothes. She would have loved a shower but there was too much to do.

Slicking her damp hair back into a tiny, messy bun, she took up residence behind the front counter and sent AJ a text letting him know the shop was back open. Almost immediately, her phone flashed with a request to FaceTime. She tapped the 'Accept' button and waited for AJ's face to fill the screen.

"Hi, Aunt K.," he said.

"Hey. Is there something specific we need to talk about?"

"Not really. I just wanted to check in."

"Things are fine here. I should be around for the next few hours anyway."

"I mean about whatever happened this morning."

Kalina massaged the bridge of her nose. She loved her nephew and his sense of curiosity but she didn't want him to go running off with wild theories about what happened, especially when she wasn't even sure anyone else in town knew Mr. Larrabee was dead. "I know I said I'd fill you in but there aren't enough pieces for me to make sense of it right now. When I know more for certain, I'll tell you."

"It happened again, didn't it? Someone's dead and there's something weird about it." AJ's face lit up as he spoke. She thought she saw a hint of fear beneath the curious expression.

"I need you to keep this to yourself. The police are still investigating and we don't need to panic people if there's no reason. I'm sure everything will turn out fine."

AJ bit his lip and looked away from the camera. "If you say so."

"Look, you can still come by later if you want but I need to take care of things around here, okay?"

"Yeah. Okay."

The screen went dark and the connection died. Kalina set the phone down on the counter and massaged the cramp out of her hand from holding the phone steady. She hated that she couldn't give her nephew more reassurance that everything would be fine but that couldn't be helped right now. Blowing out a breath, she booted up the tablet and connected to the internet. Her first stop, logically, was Facebook. She scanned through her list of friends but Nadine didn't come up. Either she didn't have an account—unlikely even for their generation—or Kalina had never gotten around to adding her as a friend. Even if she could find a friend in common, there was only so much information she could glean from the other woman's profile and what she was searching for wasn't likely to be available to casual viewers.

Closing down the app on her tablet, she brought up a browser window and logged into the library website, quickly navigating to the periodicals and the newspaper archives. If something happened right after high school, it would have made the paper. Ellesworth was small enough that most big events—good or bad—made the front page. Unlike the last time she'd needed to do a newspaper search, the editions she needed were all digital. Biting her lip in concentration, she selected '2000-2001' editions and typed 'Larrabee' into the keyword search.

A front page article from July 2003 appeared at the top on the results page.

Local Family Rocked by Tragedy

By: Angeline Reagan, Contributing Writer

Independence Day is meant to be a celebration of our country's birth as a democracy, but for one local family, the holiday will forever be remembered as a day of loss. Coming home from a late night celebration, Edwin and Michelle Larrabee were involved in a collision that left Edwin with several lacerations and a broken arm. Unfortunately, his wife is reported to have suffered severe head trauma and is presently in the intensive care unit at Ellesworth Hospital.

The couple's nineteen-year-old daughter, Nadine, was reportedly asleep in the backseat and suffered only minor cuts and bruises. Officers on scene refused to release any information about whether Mr. Larrabee was intoxicated, however eyewitness reports note that he swerved to avoid an oncoming truck, which was driving in the wrong lane.

Kalina set her tablet down on the counter and sighed. How could she have missed something so huge? Her parents would have told her the news, right? She tried to remember if they'd let her know that Nadine's mom had been in a serious accident but she came up blank. She hit the back button and found a second reference in the last edition for July. Her chest tightened and she fought back tears as she picked up the tablet again.

Obituaries

Michelle (Marcus) Larrabee

Michelle Larrabee of Ellesworth, Massachusetts passed away on July 28, 2000 from complications after a car accident left her in a critical condition. Michelle is survived by her husband,

Edwin, and their nineteen-year-old daughter, Nadine.

Michelle was an active member in the town's annual Solstice Fair committee and served on several church boards. She had a passion for poetry and spear-headed open mic nights at the local high school. Services celebrating Michelle's life will be held at the local church on July 31, 2000.

"Oh, Nadine. I'm so sorry," Kalina whispered to the empty store.

She felt like the worst friend in the world. She'd gone off to Boston to pursue her dreams in the big city and left her best friend behind. Nadine must have felt so alone losing her mother like that. Did she blame her father even if it wasn't his fault? Could there actually be some motive Kalina hadn't considered before?

No matter how much she didn't want to admit that the girl she'd once known was capable of such a horrific act, she had to admit she didn't really know the woman she'd found sitting on the front steps. She chewed on her lower lip, debating what to do next. There was probably very little chance that Chris had already obtained useful information but that didn't mean she couldn't snoop around a little later on.

The bell above the front door rang, signaling a customer, and Kalina quickly dried her eyes and closed down the browser. The tall, burly form of Andrew Chambers loomed on the other side of the counter. He slammed down a handful of comics.

"Good morning, Mr. Chambers." She fixed him with a smile. "Can I help you with something?"

"You can stop selling this crap to my kid."

Kalina glanced down at the pile of Daredevil comics and back to Mr. Chambers. "I'm sorry you don't approve of your son's reading habits but parenting him isn't my job."

"He's supposed to be reading books. Not this ... stuff."

Kalina cleared her throat and leaned forward on her elbows. "Maybe you should be happy he's reading anything at all rather than spending his time stuck online. You may not think he's learning but he is. And if what he's buying makes you uncomfortable, talk to him. But as long as he's not buying issues that are too highly rated for his age group, I'm going to keep selling them."

She spun around on her stool and straightened the hem of her blouse. "If that's all, I have some inventory I need to get to. Have a nice day."

Mr. Chambers grabbed the comics and with a scowl he stalked out, slamming the front door behind him. Kalina shook her head and let out a slow breath. "Jerk."

5

Morning quickly turned to late afternoon and Kalina found herself organizing the game room for the third time in as many hours. Even on slow days she could usually occupy herself with more success. Out front the bell rang again and she straightened.

"It's just me, Aunt K.," AJ called.

She met him halfway between the front counter and the game room. "It's pretty dead right now, kid. There's not much for you to do."

"Yeah, I know. I just wanted to ask you something. Before you say no, I've already cleared it with Mom."

"Okay. What is it?"

"How would you feel about hiring me for like after school and weekends? Once I'm sixteen I mean. I could help with inventory or supervise the game room."

"I don't know, AJ."

"Please. This was always supposed to be a family business, right? And I've helped out before over the summer."

She nodded. "Yes." She raked her fingers through her hair. "I'll think about it."

AJ pulled her into a hug and she returned the gesture. "You're the best aunt ever."

She laughed a little. "Thanks. You know, we could test it out right now if you want. I don't expect anyone to come in but I have to run an errand."

"I do know how to operate a cash register. I promise I won't burn the place down."

"Okay. Fine. Text me if there are any problems." Kalina grabbed her keys from below the counter and headed for her car. She could easily walk to her destination but the heat was still too oppressive.

Twenty minutes later, she pulled into the parking lot at the police precinct, a bag of take-out Chinese in the passenger seat. She'd called the hospital while waiting for her order but the nurse on duty had said Nadine was still sedated. That worried her. Sure, Nadine had been upset at the scene but anyone would be. She tried to shake the feeling as she headed inside.

"Evening, Kal." Jimmy greeted her from his post at the front desk.

She stopped and rested the bag on the desk. "Hey. So you're back from the scene?"

The precinct was fairly deserted but he still leaned in close. "Yeah. Man I'm glad they covered the body before I got there. Just seeing what was left made me almost lose my breakfast. I never saw a dead body before." He paled and swallowed loudly. "I mean I know we're trained to deal with these things but it's different thinking about it and doing it, you know?"

Kalina nodded. "I bet. Did you find any-thing ... interesting?"

He smiled. He was young—maybe 25—and eager to please. She felt only a tiny twinge of guilt at playing on his insecurity. "Well, I'm just writing up my report now." He looked down at the screen in front of him. "Oh, yeah the weird thing was the way he landed."

"Really?"

"I think the medical examiner is going to do a test to see if he was pushed."

Interesting, indeed.

She scanned the rest of the bull pen and spotted Chris bent over a file. "Well, good luck with the report, Jimmy." She made a show of picking up the take-out. "I'd better get this over to Detective Harper."

Jimmy beamed back at her. "You have a good night."

Kalina waved goodbye and crossed the bull pen to Chris's desk. He rubbed at the nape of his neck as he studied a file in front of him. Plopping down in the empty chair across from him she cleared her throat. "Hey."

He jumped a little at her greeting but he smiled back at her. "I didn't know you were coming down."

"I thought I'd surprise you. And—" Kalina opened the bag and pulled out a container of pork fried rice "—I wanted to make sure you didn't forget to eat."

Chris chuckled and closed the file. "Thanks. That's really sweet of you. I'll go see if I can find some plates."

While he disappeared into the small kitchen, Kalina unpacked the rest of the containers and plastic utensils. Casting a furtive glance around the rest of the bull pen, she reached over and opened the file he'd been reading: Nadine's medical history. She'd been institutionalized for six months about five years ago. First thing in the morning she was making a trip back to the hospital to have a chat with her old friend.

"Found them!" Chris called.

Kalina quickly replaced the file and took a steadying breath as he returned. She dished out some Kung Pao Chicken onto her plate along with a teriyaki beef strip and some rice. Chris loaded his plate down and leaned back in his chair.

"So, how was the rest of your day?" he asked around a mouthful of food.

"Pretty slow. Andrew Chambers came by to try to chew me out about his son reading comics."

"I hope he wasn't rude."

"Oh, he was but I told him he should actually parent the kid and talk to him if he didn't like what his son was reading."

"Good for you."

"And I'm thinking of hiring AJ on to help out around the shop after school once he's sixteen. He seems really excited."

"I think he just likes hanging out with his cool aunt in nerd heaven."

"Probably." She briefly turned her attention back to the food on her plate. "Can I ask you something?"

"Sure."

"Nadine's mom... I had no idea she'd died."

"Yeah. From what I heard it was pretty rough. Her dad was pretty broken up about it after she passed."

"I can imagine. Did they ever figure out what happened? With the accident I mean."

Chris's brow furrowed. "I don't know what you mean."

"Well, I read an article that said it might

have been another driver's fault. Or Mr. Larrabee might have been drunk."

"I'm not really sure."

"Don't you think it might be important?"

"Maybe. But, Kal, that's my job to figure out."

"I know... Sorry. I was just trying to help."

"Even if it means implicating a good friend in a murder?"

Kalina sniffled. "Yes."

The conversation fizzled out and Kalina was grateful. She wanted to just enjoy her boyfriend's company and pretend for a short while that everything was fine and the lives of the people around them weren't falling apart at the seams. She was so absorbed in the moment that she didn't hear the footsteps until Jimmy peered over Chris's shoulder at the leftovers.

"They always give you an extra fortune cookie," he said and snapped up a plastic-wrapped cookie without asking permission. "Oh, boss, here's my report from earlier."

Chris took the report and slid it on top of Nadine's medical history without looking at it. He turned to the officer and gave him an expectant look. Jimmy blissfully ignored him as he fussed with opening the plastic and cracking open the cookie.

"Hmm—" Jimmy studied the fortune "—that's not really a fortune. I mean everyone could have good luck this week, right?"

"Uh, Jimmy, you need to get back to the desk now," Chris said.

"Oh right. Sorry! You guys are on a date. I'm such an idiot I should have realized."

Kalina tried to give him an understanding smile but devolved into a fit of giggles as soon as he was out of earshot. "He's like a lost puppy sometimes," she said.

"I hate to admit it but you're right. He means well, he's just a little clueless sometimes."

The tension over Nadine's situation lifted for a moment and Kalina picked up one of the remaining fortune cookies. She popped the plastic and cracked the cookie. She studied the tiny slip of paper with mild amusement that quickly turned sour. 'An old friend will come into your life in an unexpected way'.

"Get something good?" Chris leaned over to take the paper from her.

"Just hitting a little close to home. I'm sure it's just a coincidence." She cleared her throat. "I should get going. I'm sure you have lots to get done before the end of your shift, too."

She gathered up the empty food containers and tossed them in the trash nearby. Before Chris could say anything she was halfway to the front door. She gave Jimmy a hasty wave before she braved the evening heat. Footsteps pounded on the pavement behind her and she slowed down.

"Kal, wait a minute," Chris said and spun

her around to face him. "It's just a fortune cookie. It's not meant to be serious."

She let out a huff of annoyance. "I know that. It's just been a long day. That's all."

He tucked a few strands of hair behind her ear and leaned in for a kiss. "Good night."

6

Kalina headed to the hospital just after eight the next morning. The shop remained closed with a sign indicating that the closure was due to inventory. It was an outright lie but she could handle a little lost business. Nadine was more important. As she waited to check in at the nurse's station she wondered why, after all these years, she felt so compelled to be there for Nadine. As she headed down the east wing to a private room, she realized she felt guilty. She needed to apologize for letting them drift so far apart during college. Sure, Nadine could have reached out, too, but given her current situation, Kalina was more than willing to heap the extra blame on herself.

Taking a left turn at the next junction, Kalina finally found Nadine's room. It was a single occupant room with a view of the distant shoreline. Nadine sat on the bed, staring out the window. She looked calmer than she'd been the day before and Kalina breathed a sigh of relief that her friend was awake and alert. She knocked on the doorframe and Nadine turned with a ghost of a smile on her lips.

"Can I come in?" Kalina asked, standing in the doorway.

"Sure." Her voice was stronger than it had been the day before, too.

Kalina crossed the room in two big strides and she settled in a chair under the flat-screen TV mounted to the wall. Nadine tugged at a few curls and kept her gaze on the floor. Awkward silence filled the room. Kalina wasn't sure what to say.

"How are you?"

Nadine shrugged one shoulder. "They are letting me leave today. I guess that's good."

"Yeah, definitely."

"I can't go home. Not after... I just keep seeing him on driveway."

Kalina reached out and took Nadine's hand in hers. "You can stay with me if you want. I have a free futon."

"You don't have to do that. This isn't your mess."

"You're my friend. At least I hope you still are and I want to help. And once the house isn't a crime scene anymore I can go pick up some clothes and stuff for you."

"You'd do that?"

"Of course."

Nadine squeezed Kalina's hand. "Thanks, Kal." She glanced over her shoulder towards the empty doorway. "The nurse said she'd be back with discharge papers but that was like twenty minutes ago."

"I'm sure you'll be out of here before you know it." Footsteps echoed down the hallway, growing louder. "See, I bet that's the nurse now."

Her shoulders fell a little bit when Chris appeared in the doorway. He raised an eyebrow at her but said nothing. Nadine pulled her knees up to her chest in a protective posture and didn't let go of Kalina's hand.

"How are you feeling, Miss Larrabee?" he asked.

"You can call me Nadine. We all know each other," Nadine said.

Chris cleared his throat. "All right, how are you doing, Nadine?"

"I'm okay. They're discharging me now."

"That's good to hear." He turned to Kalina. "I trust you're here just as a friend."

Kalina nodded. "Nothing more, I swear."

"I need to ask you some questions about your father's death, Nadine. I'd like you to come down to the station this afternoon."

"Do I need a lawyer or something?"

"That's up to you. But right now you are the only witness to what happened and we need to get your statement."

"I'll make sure she gets there." Kalina released Nadine's hand and stood up. "Can I talk to you for a minute, Detective?"

He gestured towards the hallway and they stepped out of the room. "What's wrong, Kal?"

"So she's a *witness* now?"

"She's always been a witness. She might be a suspect, too, but right now there's nothing to support charging her."

Kalina studied his face for any sign that he was bluffing but she couldn't find any. Maybe he really didn't have anything. But Jimmy seemed certain the forensic team had been to the house so they had to have discovered something. Chris lifted her chin so they were eye to eye.

"I'm doing everything I can to figure this out. I just need you to be a little patient. Can you do that?"

"Yes." She fought the urge to lean in for a kiss. "What time do you want her there for the interview?"

"Bring her by around three."

Before she could reply, a nurse in pale pink scrubs approached with a clipboard and some paperwork. They moved out of her way and waited while Nadine signed the forms. The sound of a heart monitor went dead and Nadine appeared with the forms in hand.

"Can we get out of here?"

The three of them walked back to the main entrance of the hospital and out to the parking lot. Kalina and Nadine parted ways with Chris as he climbed into a marked police cruiser and pulled away. Kalina unlocked her car and they settled in.

"So, is there something going on with you and Chris?" Nadine asked as Kalina started the engine.

"We've been seeing each other since June."

"I guess first loves do come back to you if you let them free."

Kalina smiled a toothy grin. "I guess so."

"Thanks again for doing this," Nadine said, rubbing at her forehead.

Kalina reached over to pat the woman on the shoulder. They would get through this together. She did her best to squash her doubts about Nadine's innocence in the whole mess. Nadine needed her support right now, not judgment.

"Do you mind if we stop by the shop for a bit?" Kalina asked as she eased to a stop at a stop sign. Geeks and Things sat half a block up on Main Street.

"Shop?"

"I took over my dad's comic book shop after he died a few months back."

"Oh, I didn't realize. Sorry about your dad."

"That's okay. I didn't know your mom had died, either. I'm sorry I wasn't around for you back then."

"It would have been nice to have my best friend there but ... people drift apart after high school. And I could have made more of an effort."

Kalina smiled at her friend. Kids had it so much easier these days with Facebook keeping everyone connected. The whole phenomenon had been just a little behind their college experience. "I want you to know I'm here for you now." She accelerated through the intersection and pulled in behind the store. She'd spotted a few people on the sidewalk, lounging by the front door. The late opening wasn't hurting business after all.

"So did you want to take over the store

after your dad passed?" Nadine asked as they climbed out and Kalina pulled her keys out of her pocket.

"Yeah. I ended up going to grad school for business. It's kind of a dream come true, honestly. I was always more into all the nerdy stuff than Jillian and I didn't realize it until recently, but I love being able to keep the family business alive. It kind of feels like my dad's still around a little bit."

Nadine nodded wordlessly and waited while Kalina unlocked the back door. They made their way to the front of the store through the game room. Kalina moved with quick steps to the front door, unlocking it and pulling it open. "Come on in."

Customers lined up in front of the counter and Nadine stood off to the side, watching intently. Kalina darted to the back to retrieve their waiting orders. Thank goodness none of them were waiting on Valiant Comics. She hadn't had a chance to sort through the new inventory yet. She'd gotten through the first customer when the bell above the door rang and Andrew Chambers walked in. Kalina suppressed a groan and motioned Nadine to join her from where she was lurking in the back.

"Can you run a register?"

"Yeah. Why?"

She nodded toward Mr. Chambers. "I need to take care of something. Everything is written on the folders. Thanks so much."

Kalina blew out a breath and motioned for Mr. Chambers to follow her into the game room. She braced herself for another confrontation but it seemed it might not come. He shuffled into the room behind her, hands in his pockets and his gaze cast downward.

He cleared his throat and said, "I wanted to apologize for my behavior yesterday."

"Oh." She hadn't been expecting an apology.

"It's just"—he looked around the room—"Kevin's grades weren't that great this past school year and I thought maybe it was be-cause of the comics. But I did like you said and talked to him. It wasn't a fun talk, believe me. But he's been having issues since his mom left."

Kalina's expression softened. "I'm so sorry to hear that."

He shrugged off her concern. "It was a long time coming. I guess I'm not so good at all the emotional stuff. Look, do you think maybe when school starts he could hang out here after school and do his homework? He's promised he'll do it."

"He's welcome to come by."

Mr. Chambers smiled. "Thanks. And, again, I'm sorry I lost it on you."

"I'm used to it."

"Hey, Kal. I need some help," Nadine called.

"I'll let you get back to work."

Kalina offered her hand to Mr. Chambers. He shook it and headed out of the shop.

Kalina rejoined Nadine at the counter and helped her sort out a glitch with Square. Finally, the shop was quiet again. Kalina fiddled with the tablet for a few minutes before she set it aside and leaned on her elbows. "Can I ask you something?"

"Yeah."

"Do you remember the accident? I read what was in the paper yesterday but it seemed kind of vague."

Nadine's cheeks paled and she slumped onto the stool. She took several deep breaths. "We were at a Fourth of July party. I didn't want to go but my mom made me. I don't think she wanted to be alone with my dad. He'd been drinking but refused to give Mom the keys."

"So he was drunk. There was no truck in the wrong lane."

"There might have been. It was late and I was half-asleep when it happened." She closed her eyes tight as if trying to remember that night. "I can still hear the tires and brakes squealing and the sound of the airbags deploying. The rest is kind of a blur though."

"Did they test your dad's blood alcohol level? I mean even if there was a truck he shouldn't have been driving when he was drunk."

"They probably did but I don't know what happened. All I know is no one wanted to charge him with anything. He was buddies with the chief of police at the time and he just looked the other way."

"Police corruption at its best."

"Yeah. I heard about what happened with Dan Cahill. That's crazy."

"Yeah, it was. I was there when he was arrested."

Nadine let out a nervous hiccup of laughter. "You were? Why?"

"I was sort of unofficially helping Chris out with the case. Not that he'd ever admit to that."

"Do you think you could come with me to the police station?"

"Yeah, of course. I don't think he'll let me sit in with you on the interview but I could probably wait outside."

"I need to call Adam."

Kalina cocked her head in curiosity. "Who is Adam?"

"My boyfriend. He's a lawyer. I think I need one."

"Chris just wants your statement about what happened."

"I think I might have done something, Kal. It wouldn't be the first time."

"What do you mean?"

"Not many people know but I was locked up in a psych ward for about six months. My father had them convinced I was bipolar. I'm not. I know I'm not but even without a law degree I know that looks suspicious. I don't speak to my father for years after I'm committed and then we reconnect and he ends up dead. That doesn't look good for me, Kal."

"I'm sure you didn't do anything."

"The night's kind of fuzzy to be honest. But what if I did do something?"

"But you said you aren't bipolar."

"No, but he drugged me before. What if he did it again and I blacked or something?"

"Could you really have pushed him out a window, even if you were drugged?"

"Maybe—" she dug the heels of her hands into her eyes "—I need to call Adam and let him know what's happening."

"You can borrow my phone if you want." Kalina unlocked her phone and slid it across the counter.

Nadine picked it up and entered a number before hitting 'Call' and disappearing to the game room for some privacy. Kalina's stomach lurched at Nadine's revelation. She hadn't wanted to believe her friend could be responsible for killing a man but Nadine was right.

There was definitely some motive. And if they were the only two people in the house then she had no alibi and she'd been sedated with enough drugs at the hospital it could have messed up any toxicology test the doctors ran. Maybe eavesdropping on Chris's interview would shed some more light on things.

7

At ten minutes until three, Kalina and Nadine pulled into the parking lot of the police station. A car Kalina didn't recognize pulled in behind them and a tall man climbed out. Nadine lunged out of the passenger seat and threw herself into his arms. He held her tight and kissed her forehead. From her spot by the driver side door, Kalina could make out that he had a few strands of gray in his otherwise full head of dark brown hair. He could have been their age or a little older. She tried to not intrude on their private moment. After Nadine finally relinquished her grip around his torso, he closed the distance between the two cars and extended his hand to Kalina.

"Adam Shepard, Nadine's boyfriend."

"Kalina Greystone. Friend. I also hear you're an attorney."

"Yeah. One of the partners in my firm helped Nadine out a few years ago. That's how we met."

Nadine stayed close to Adam's side as they headed into the precinct. Jimmy was no longer at the reception desk. He was bent over something at Chris's desk.

"Hey, Jimmy, is Chris here?" Kalina called.

The young officer jumped and turned to face them. "Oh, uh... Hi, Kal. Yeah he's around here somewhere."

"Can you let him know that Nadine Larrabee is here for her interview?"

"Right. I'll let him know right now." He hurried off toward the chief's office.

The department was even more short-staffed since they hadn't gotten around to replacing Captain Cahill. No one seemed to want the job. She suspected they would eventually have to bring in someone else from outside of the town to oversee things. Behind her, she could hear Adam and Nadine speaking in hushed voices but they stopped the moment Chris appeared.

"Thank you for coming in. If you'll follow me." He pointed to the only interrogation room the department had.

Kalina stayed where she was, dutifully not butting in on her boyfriend's job. She smiled politely as Jimmy walked past her and sat down at the front desk. She gave Chris a thumbs up when he gestured for her to stay put. With a quick glance over her shoulder to make sure Jimmy was distracted, she settled in at Chris's desk and watched the interview on the small monitor nearby.

"Miss Larrabee, can you tell me what you remember from two nights ago? What were you doing at your father's house?"

Nadine crossed her arms over her chest. "We were having dinner. I'd brought Adam over to meet him. I thought maybe it was time we tried to put our differences behind us. He'd been sober for a year."

"Adam Shepard, your attorney?"

"I'm here in my official capacity as Nadine's counsel," Adam said.

Chris scribbled something on his notepad. "So you had dinner."

"Yes. It ... wasn't the greatest meal. I don't think he really liked that I had a boyfriend."

Chris nodded. "Then what happened?"

Nadine shrugged. "We were going to leave but my father insisted I stay. Adam left. He had to prepare for a trial the next day. I thought things were going to be okay but then my father poured himself a drink. I didn't have anywhere else to go so I made some tea and went to bed."

"So you didn't argue with your father about him breaking his sobriety?"

"No. I don't think so. It's kind of hazy after I went to bed. I thought I heard arguing but I must have been dreaming. Then I woke up and found him the next morning, lying in the driveway."

"But no one else was in the house at the time. Just the two of you?"

Nadine glanced over at Adam who said nothing. "Yes. Just the two of us."

Chris flipped open a file—likely Nadine's medical history—and paged through it. "I see you were hospitalized for psychiatric concerns a few years ago."

"I'm not crazy. We proved it. He was drugging me to make me look like I was bipolar."

"Why would he do that to his own daughter?"

"Because he's a cruel man. He knew his side of the family had a history so it would look credible."

"I still don't understand why he would want to fake a mental illness. What reason would he have?"

"Detective, I don't see how this is relevant," Adam chimed in.

"Just getting all the facts on the table, Counselor. Your client's relationship with her father, both presently and in the past, may speak to any potential motive."

"Motive? So now she's a suspect?"

Kalina knew where this was going and, as much as she wanted to know what happened between Nadine and her father, it wasn't going to come out now that Adam was on the defense. Instead, she turned her attention to the files littering Chris's desk. His normally clean and organized workspace had been overtaken by the case at hand. She flipped open the top folder and almost wished she hadn't. A close-up photo of Mr. Larrabee's face, bruised and bloody, greeted her. Once the shock wore off, she took a closer look. In all of the commotion of finding Nadine two days ago, she hadn't really noticed that he'd landed face down on the pavement. No wonder Jimmy said the medical examiner thought he'd been pushed.

She closed the folder and spun around in the chair. Jimmy drummed his fingers on the keyboard at the front desk, clearly bored. Hoping she could get lucky twice in two days, she ambled over to him and put on her best flirty smile. "Hey there. Can I ask you something?"

Jimmy sighed and looked toward the interrogation. "Man, I wish I could be in there. I want to make detective someday. I could be learning so much from Chris."

"I'm sure you'll get there. Hell, you'll probably end up running this place one day."

Jimmy blushed and finger-combed his

hair nervously. "Thanks. Did you need something?"

"Yeah, actually I was hoping you could help me out. I'm sure Chris doesn't want Nadine going back to the house. But I promised I'd pick up her stuff for her. Overnight bag. That sort of thing. Do you know if forensics has cleared the scene?"

"Oh, yeah they did that yesterday. Wasn't much there."

"Do you think you could go with me? I don't feel comfortable going alone."

"Sure thing, Kal."

A sound from the monitor nearby drew Kalina's attention back to the interrogation. Chris pushed an evidence photo of what looked like rope across the table. "Have you seen this before, Miss Larrabee?"

Nadine shook her head. "No. Why?"

"We found it in your father's study. The lab is running it for fingerprints right now. What do you think we'll find?"

"That's enough, Detective. If you have something to charge my client with, do it; otherwise, we're leaving." Adam stood up and took Nadine by the elbow, guiding her away from the table and towards the door.

"I know you aren't local anymore, Nadine, but don't leave town," Chris said and gathered up his materials.

Kalina darted from Chris's desk and raced to stand near Jimmy. He didn't react to her sudden presence, which was a blessing. Nadine and Adam appeared and made a bee line for the door, not bothering to stop. But as they passed, Kalina overheard Adam tell Nadine she could stay with him at the only hotel in town. So at least she knew where they were going. Chris appeared next, making his way to his desk and tossing the files on top of the ever-growing pile. He rubbed at the back of his neck—a clear sign of stress—and headed for the front of the building as well.

"I need some air," he announced to no one in particular and disappeared from view.

Jimmy rounded the front desk and held up the keys to the squad car parked in the front lot. "Ready to go?"

8

The trip to the Larrabee house was surprisingly short. There was little need for conversation until Jimmy cut the engine at the end of the driveway. He pulled the keys from the ignition and nearly dropped them between his feet. Kalina pretended not to notice his nerves.

"You okay, Jimmy?"

"Yeah. Just ... being back here kind of freaks me out a little. Don't tell Detective Harper."

Kalina mimed locking her lips and throwing away the key. "Your secret is safe with me. Besides, being here kind of freaks me out, too."

Together they exited the squad car and marched up to the front door. It was still un-locked. Jimmy nudged it open with his forearm and stepped inside first. The house didn't feel any different than any other house. Somehow she'd expected it to be marked by death with a draft or scent of blood. It was a normal house that brought back memories of spending afternoons with Nadine doing homework in high school.

"I think the bedroom is on the second floor," Jimmy announced but stayed at the foot of the stairs.

"I remember," Kalina murmured and started up the staircase.

She stopped on the second floor landing and just took in the décor. It hadn't changed in fifteen years, except for a picture of Nadine at their high school graduation. She looked so happy and full of potential. So much had happened to dampen her spirit. It wasn't fair. With a soft sigh, Kalina crept up to the third floor to take a look around. From what she remembered of the layout and the position of Mr. Larrabee's body, she ignored the master bedroom and half bathroom and headed straight for the study. It was a mess with papers strewn across the desk. There were scuff marks on the hardwood floor and the desk chair had been turned over. It certainly appeared as though there had been a struggle. Bending down to right the chair, Kalina noticed what looked like bloodstains on the tan leather armrests.

"What happened in here?"

Sidestepping the chair, she approached the window and peered down at the driveway below. From this angle she had no doubt a fall from this height could kill a person. Had the police done their test yet? Surely that would give Chris an idea of whether Nadine was involved or not. She longed to know more about what happened between father and daughter that could lead to something like this. A floorboard creaked behind her and she spun, her right hand pressed to her chest in surprise. Jimmy stood in the doorway.

"I thought the bedroom was on the second floor?"

Kalina caught her breath and nodded. "It is... I just got curious. I know it sounds awful but I wanted to see it for myself. Don't tell anyone, please?"

Jimmy nodded and she followed him back down to the second floor landing. He waited patiently outside Nadine's room as she gathered up the clothes strewn on the floor, tossing them in the overnight duffle bag laid beneath the window. Nadine really hadn't been planning on staying long. The bed had not been touched; the covers still haphazardly kicked to one side. A half-empty teacup sat on the nightstand on the left side of the bed. Curiosity got the best of her and she picked it up.

"Find something?" Jimmy called.

"Maybe. Did anyone examine this tea?"

Jimmy scratched at the stubble on his chin. "Um... I don't think so. Why would they do that? Mr. Larrabee wasn't killed in here."

Kalina bit her lip, unsure how much to divulge about her earlier conversation with her friend. "Nadine said she thought her father might have drugged her the night he died. Maybe some of whatever he used is still in the tea."

Jimmy's cheeks burned bright red in embarrassment. "Oh ... right. Like with Mrs. Davies."

"Exactly."

Jimmy pulled out his phone and disappeared back down to the first floor. Kalina took one last cursory look around the room before joining him. Neither of them had touched the tea and so she assumed chain of evidence hadn't been ruined. He hung up just as she got to the bottom of the stairs.

"They said I should bag it myself and bring it to the station. They'll have someone pick it up there to run some tests."

"Can you do that?"

He puffed out his chest. "Yeah. Detective Harper always makes us keep extra gloves and evidence bags in the squad car just in case. Us being such a small department and all."

"I'll wait here while you do that," Kalina said.

Jimmy hurried out to the car and returned moments later with blue gloves and a clear baggie marked 'EVIDENCE- ELLESWORTH PD' on it. True to her word, she waited outside while he headed upstairs to retrieve the teacup and its potentially-drugged contents. As she waited, the third story window drew her attention. Nadine didn't have time to wait for a lengthy police procedure to determine her guilt or innocence. Kalina would find a way to test the theory of whether Mr. Larrabee was pushed or not.

"What's going on out here?" An older man's voice pulled her from her thoughts.

She turned her attention to the man standing just over the property line to the next house over. Mr. Martin Beech had lived there for as long as Kalina had been alive and friends with Nadine. He was a bit odd but harmless enough.

"Oh, hi, Mr. Beech. You probably saw all the emergency personnel here the other day for Mr. Larrabee." Two days seemed more than enough time for the news to begin spreading. She was quite impressed that people weren't spreading rumors already.

"Course I did. With all the racket they were making, how could I not?"

Kalina set down the duffle bag on the front steps and closed the distance between them. "Did you see anything strange the night before?"

Mr. Beech waved his hand dismissively. "I don't like to pry."

"Oh, of course not. I didn't mean to imply you were prying. But you are pretty observant from what I remember. Nadine and I couldn't sneak anything past you when we were kids."

Mr. Beech grinned, his dentures gleaming. "You girls were always a handful. But I do like to keep an eye on the neighborhood."

Flattery at its best. "I'm sure Nadine would be really grateful if you did happen to see something the other night. She's really torn up about her father's death."

"Oh, sure. Poor thing. You know, it was kind of a surprise to see her around. It'd been maybe five or six years since I'd seen her at the house. She seemed subdued when I said hello. Like she had something else on her mind. But whatever it was, she must have gotten over it because she stayed the night."

Kalina leaned in conspiratorially. "You

don't think she had anything to do with his death, do you?"

"Little Nadine? That girl couldn't hurt a fly. You know, now that you mention it, I did notice something odd."

"What?"

"Well, I've had trouble sleeping the last few nights. The heat just doesn't agree with me. So I was up around two in the morning." He paused, seeming to collect his thoughts. "Yes, it was two. I went downstairs to get a glass of warm milk when I saw a car."

"A car? Did you recognize it or the person driving?"

"Well, it looked like the car Nadine showed up in earlier. I guess the fellow she was with had left but it looked like he came back. Now, I don't mean to be nosy but that fellow went inside and then maybe ten minutes later came back out and left the door wide open!"

"So there was someone else in the house besides Nadine and her father."

"Saw him clear as day."

"Did Nadine introduce him to you earlier?"

Mr. Beech shook his head. "I'm afraid not." His face lit up. "But I did write down the license plate. I thought it was rather suspicious it being so late at night and all. I'll go get it."

Before Kalina could ask any more questions, Mr. Beech tottered off towards his front door and Jimmy appeared, carefully cradling the cup in both hands.

"Sorry I took so long. Wanted to make sure it didn't spill."

"That's okay. I was just having a nice conversation with Edwin Beech. I think he might have seen something."

"Seen what?"

"A car coming and leaving the house between two o'clock and two fifteen the morning Mr. Larrabee died."

Jimmy did a little hop of excitement at the news and tiny droplets of tea sloshed against the clear plastic. His cheeks reddened again and he walked, stiff-legged, down to the squad car to secure the bag. Mr. Beech reappeared and waved a slip of paper in Kalina's face.

"Here it is."

She plucked it from his outstretched fingers. "Thanks. You've been a huge help."

"You tell Nadine I'm thinking of her."

"I will." Kalina retrieved the overnight bag and walked down the driveway to join Jimmy. She handed him the paper with the license plate number and they both climbed in.

"Boy did we get lucky you happened to strike up a conversation with him," Jimmy said and nestled the teacup into one of the cup holders. He punched the license plate number into the minicomputer synced to the DMV database and let out a long whistle as the computer went 'ping' with a result.

"What is it?" Kalina tried to read the result but Jimmy blocked the screen.

He hit speed dial on his cell phone. Whoever he was calling picked up after the first ring. "Detective Harper, it's Jimmy. I think you might want to bring Adam Shepard back in for some questioning."

9

Kalina stared open-mouthed as Jimmy repeated the information. She had no problem letting Chris think it was all Jimmy's doing. After all, she'd said she would keep out of the investigation, not do their job for them.

"I understand. I'll see you back at the station, Sir." Jimmy ended the call and looked at Kalina. "Nadine's lawyer boyfriend came back that night. Wonder why she didn't say anything before?"

Kalina shrugged. "Maybe she didn't know. If she really was drugged then she wouldn't remember him coming in or out."

Jimmy ran a hand over his hair. "Detective Harper wants me back at the station. Can I drop you somewhere?"

"The shop would be fine." She really wanted him to take her to the motel but that would have looked suspicious. If Chris didn't want Jimmy to pick up Adam from the motel for questioning, then Chris was likely getting the lawyer to the station under false pretenses. She might have some time to get to the motel first.

Five minutes later, Jimmy pulled up to the shop. AJ stood outside, arms crossed over his chest. He did not look happy. Kalina climbed out of the passenger side with the overnight bag in hand and waited for the squad car to pull away.

"Do you have any idea what time it is?" her nephew asked with mock annoyance.

"Yeah, yeah. Come on. You wanted to know what's been going on; well, it's time I filled you in. I'm going to need your help anyway."

They headed inside and AJ flipped the front sign to 'Closed'. He pointed to the bag but Kalina tossed it aside.

"An old friend of mine's father died two days ago. It looks like it was murder and Nadine is the prime suspect. There was some bad blood between her and her father but I'm not sure about the whole story. We just found out someone else was there the night her father died. Chris is investigating."

"What do you need from me?"

"I need you to look up how to test if a person was pushed or fell from a high altitude."

"You mean the 'Push Jump Fall' test."

Kalina furrowed her brow. "Where'd you learn that?"

AJ grinned. "Heroes."

Kalina let out a soft laugh. "Of course. Now, I need you to look up how to test it and see if you can find a dummy we can use."

"I know just where to look."

"You can't tell anyone what you need it for. Chris can't find out we're doing this."

AJ nodded. "So while I'm doing this, what are you doing?"

'I'm going to the motel and, hopefully, I can get Nadine to fill in some of the blanks about her past. It might be the only way we can figure out what really happened to her father."

"You can count on me, Aunt K."

She pulled her nephew into a brief, one-armed hug. "I knew I could. Now, call me when you've got everything. And remember—"

"I know. Don't tell anyone what we're doing."

Kalina picked up the overnight bag and headed out across town. She supposed she was lucky that Ellesworth was small enough to only have one motel. If anyone came to stay in the area, they usually stayed in Salem and drove down to the beaches here. She reached the parking lot some ten minutes later to find only one car there bearing a familiar license plate. Adam hadn't left yet. What was Chris waiting for? She paid the front desk a quick visit to get the right room number and walked down three doors and stopped. She could hear voices coming from inside the room.

"I don't understand why he wants to talk to you alone," Nadine said.

"Don't worry about it. Everything is going to be fine. I promise."

"You're hiding something. I can tell. What is it?"

"Nadine, just let me worry about it. I'm looking out for you."

Kalina raised her hand to knock when the door flew inward and she nearly collided with Adam.

"Sorry!" she said and stepped out of his way.

"I didn't see you there," he said and headed for his car.

Nadine sat on one of the small twin beds with her knees drawn up to her chest. She looked paler than she had two days before when her father's death was fresh in her mind. Her hair was damp and hung around her face in stringy clumps. Adam had probably gotten the call when she was still in the shower. Kalina stayed in the doorway for a moment longer to be sure Nadine registered her presence. Then she crossed the threshold and set the bag on the floor.

"Hey, how are you holding up?"

Nadine scrubbed at her face and let out a long sigh. "Honestly, I don't know what to think anymore. Detective Harper just called Adam down to the station for some questions but he didn't want me there. He wouldn't say anything else."

Kalina just nodded. She didn't want to admit she'd overheard part of their conversation. Instead, she sat on the other bed and said, "I'm sure if either of them have anything to tell you, they will." Should she say anything about Adam returning in the middle of the night?

"I wish I could remember something ... anything."

"Was there anything you didn't tell Detective Harper in your interview?"

"Like what?"

"I don't know. The reason your father drugged you all those years ago."

"God, you think I did it! You think I had a motive." Nadine jumped from the bed and took a defensive posture.

"No, of course I don't." Kalina held her hands up in front of her. "I am just trying to understand how the family I knew growing up could be torn apart so violently. What happened?"

Nadine turned to face Kalina, resting her chin in her hand. "I guess it started after I turned eighteen. My parents needed to redo their wills to get rid of the need for a guardian or something. They ended up waiting an extra year. I'm not sure why. I didn't know the details but my dad got really upset that my mother was keeping the house only in her name and she was passing it to me when I turned 25. It was supposed to be held by the estate lawyer until then."

"What's so special about the house?"

She shrugged. "It's been in the family for a long time. I think my mom wanted to keep it in her side of the family. They had a pretty big knockdown, drag out fight over it right after I got home from school for the semester in June. He insisted on going to the party on the fourth of July. My mother didn't want to go. She didn't tell me but I could tell he'd been drinking more often. He wasn't the same. Always on edge and angry." Tears shone in her eyes and she tried to blink them away. "I wish she'd just given him the damn house. Maybe then he wouldn't have insisted on going to the stupid party."

"So you blamed him for what happened to your mom." It came out as more of a statement than a question.

"Maybe. I think I resented him for being so obsessed with the house. You know, that's why he drugged me and had me committed."

Kalina scratched her head, trying to follow the logic. "To get the house?"

"Yes. There was some legal loophole that said he could get control of the deed if I was declared legally incompetent. But he waited until after I turned 25 so it was legally in my name so he could force feed me whatever drugs he thought would help make his case." Her tone turned bitter. "He gave me downers so that I spiraled into a massive depression and then he gave me psychotropic pills to make me look manic. He kept giving them to me until one day I just lost it and started hitting him. He called the police and they dragged me off to the psych ward at Salem Hospital. I rotted there for six months before Adam and one of his partners figured out what was going on and got me released."

"You were able to prove it all?"

"I even tried to sue him but the judge wanted it settled out of court. He never came out and said it, but I think he felt it was just too messy. I got some restitution financially and a restraining order."

"If you had a restraining order, why did you go to see him and have dinner?"

"I let it lapse about a year ago. Adam thought it might be good to reconcile, or at least try to put the past behind us. He said there was no point in letting it eat away at our happiness."

Kalina did her best to stifle a bitter laugh of her own. "You know, I think maybe you were drugged this time, too."

"So you believe me?"

"I found the teacup and the lab is running it. And there was someone else there in the house that night."

"Someone else? How do you know that?"

It was time to spill the beans. "When I went to get your stuff from the house I ran into your neighbor, Mr. Beech. He was rather chatty. He said that that night, around two, he saw someone show up to the house and then leave a little while later."

"Who?"

"Adam."

"No, that can't be."

"Mr. Beech wrote down the license plate and Jimmy ran it. It belonged to Adam's car. I think that's why Chris wanted to talk to him alone."

Nadine scooped up the room key and headed for the door. "We have to get there now. I need to know what's happening!"

"Slow down, Nadine. We can't do anything."

"If he tells Detective Harper anything I deserve to know about it. I knew he was keeping something from me. I just didn't know it was this."

10

———

Nadine was out the door before Kalina could say anything else. They didn't have a car so it was going to be a brisk walk to the station. On the way, Kalina checked her phone for any missed calls or texts from AJ. She couldn't share that particular theory with her friend yet. She needed to process the fact that her boyfriend had been there and might have had something to do with her father's death. Was he confessing to the crime as they raced to the station? He could have certainly had enough strength and force to push a grown man out a window.

"Come on," Nadine urged as the station came into view up the street.

Kalina stowed her phone back in her pocket and trailed Nadine through the front doors. Neither of them bothered to acknowledge the officer at the front desk. Jimmy was nowhere in sight and the bull pen was empty. Chris's desk was still a mess of files and paperwork. Speaking of Chris, she spotted him on the interrogation room monitor sitting across from Adam.

"Your vehicle was seen arriving at the Larrabee residence at two in the morning and leaving at two fifteen. Want to tell me what you were doing back there in the middle of the night?"

"What evidence do you have?"

"An eye witness who recorded your license plate. Now, I'll ask you again. What were you doing back there?"

Adam let out a breath and unfolded his arms. "I didn't like how we left things with Nadine's father. I had a trial the next day but I should have insisted she come stay with me. The stories she told me were unsettling. The last time he was alone with her in that house, he purposely drugged her to get the deed to the house."

Chris opened one of the files on the table and flipped through what appeared to be court documents. "And you know all of this because of the civil suit Nadine filed against her father."

"Yes. I was part of the team that worked on her case and got her released from the hospital when it was determined she was not mentally impaired due to a disease."

"So you went back to give Mr. Larrabee a piece of your mind then?"

"No. I went back to get Nadine to go with me. When I got there she was asleep. I tried to wake her up but she wouldn't. I assumed he'd drugged her again."

"So you left her there?"

"I went to confront Edwin."

Kalina stood transfixed by the conversation. She hadn't anticipated Adam admitting he'd confronted Mr. Larrabee about what had happened with Nadine. She hadn't wanted the possibility that he was the killer to be true any more than she wanted that status to fall to her friend.

"He came back for me," Nadine whispered. "I thought I dreamed that."

"You remember him showing up?"

"A little, maybe. It honestly felt like a dream. That means the rest wasn't a dream either."

Kalina turned to look at her friend. "The rest of what?"

"I thought it was a dream. I went upstairs because I heard voices and loud noises. My father was tied to his office chair. He looked so scared. I think he told me to run but I had to untie him. Whatever else he'd done to me, he didn't deserve to be tied down. I know what that's like. Then I stumbled back down to my room. I guess Adam did wake me up."

"Did you happen to see a clock at any point during that whole thing?"

"No. Why?"

"Well, if you went and untied your father after Adam left then that doesn't make him a suspect anymore."

"But it still doesn't clear me. And why would Adam tie up my father? It was the middle of the night. I know he was drinking again but I don't think he would have done anything to really hurt me."

"I don't know but Chris needs to know what you just told me."

Nadine worried her lower lip and looked between the door to the interrogation room and the monitor. The conversation had died down. The station was eerily silent when Kalina's phone sang out the opening bars to "Hooked on Feeling"—AJ's ringtone.

"Sorry. I need to take this." She stepped away and watched as Nadine headed for the interrogation room, her shoulders squared and her head held high. "Hey, kiddo. Tell me you got what we need."

"Took longer than I thought it would but, yeah, I got it. So what's next?"

Kalina pulled her phone away from her ear to check the time. It was already well after six. "Go wait for me at the shop, around back. I'll pick you up and I'll throw in pizza when we're done."

"Sweet. Did you find out anything else?"

"I'll fill you in when I get there."

"I'll let Mom know I won't be home for dinner."

"I'll see you soon," she said and ended the call.

Nadine appeared on the monitor and took a seat beside Adam. Kalina couldn't see

Chris's facial expression but, by Adam's body language, at least one of them wasn't pleased to see Nadine waltz right in and start talking. She couldn't really blame them. If anything, it was usually the attorney barging in on the interrogation. She wanted to stay and hear what else was going on in the interrogation room but figuring out if Mr. Larrabee had been pushed or not was of more importance. She was so close to finding out what had really happened and, hopefully, clearing her friend's name. The deeper she got into the fact, the more convinced she was becoming that Nadine just didn't have it in her to kill her father, no matter what had transpired between them in the last decade. With one last glance back toward the monitor, she made the trek back to Geeks and Things.

11

———

"What took you so long?" AJ exclaimed as she rounded the back of the shop.

She let out a huff and bent over to catch her breath. Sweat glistened on her arms and she could feel beads threatening to spill from her forehead.

"Give me a break, kid. I had to walk from the other side of town. I got here as fast as I could."

He pointed to a large CPR dummy. "That will work, right?"

"It's perfect." She fanned herself with her shirt as she caught her breath. "Where'd you find it?"

"A friend was doing CPR training and lent it to me. I told them I wanted to practice in case I wanted to take the class."

"You know, should I be worried about this criminal mastermind thing you've got going?"

He laughed and grinned from ear to ear. "Just don't tell Mom."

Together, they managed to fit the dummy in the backseat of Kalina's car without it looking suspicious. The sun had begun its descent toward the horizon as she pulled out of the back lot and made her way toward Ocean Front Lane.

"So, what friend is this? Have I met them?" AJ was trying to fill the dead air between them.

"I don't think so. We hadn't spoken in a

long time. Since high school really. But the minute I saw her and realized she was in trouble, I had to help her."

"That's nuts that you would have that connection again after so long."

"It sounds cliché but it's true. Your true friends are the ones you don't see for years and you pick up right where you left off when you see them again. Of course, it doesn't usually involve murder."

"So do you think she did it?"

Kalina shook her head as she eased to a stop at stop sign. "I don't think so. I understand her relationship with her father better now but ... even with all of that behind her, she was trying to reconcile with him."

"What about the other person in the house?'

"Maybe. I am hoping this test will tell us one way or the other if Mr. Larrabee was pushed."

"Detective Harper is going to be pissed when he finds out."

"That's why we aren't telling him until we've done it. Besides, I'm sure he's got someone doing the same thing in a lab somewhere. We're just confirming results, really."

A few minutes later, she pulled up in front of the Larrabee house. She hoped Mr. Beech wasn't around. She didn't need him interfering or ratting them out to the police. Despite it being the end of the work day, the streets were mostly empty. That would work in their favor.

"Are you sure we can get in?" AJ asked as he struggled to drag the dummy out the passenger side of the backseat.

"Yes. The front door isn't locked."

"And you know this how?"

"I was here earlier with Jimmy and we didn't lock the front door when we left."

"Oh. Right."

Kalina locked the car and helped AJ carry

the dummy up the driveway to the front porch. She kept moving, forcing her nephew to keep up so he wouldn't have time to gawk at the dark stain still on the pavement. She was a little surprised no one had come to clean it up. They paused long enough for AJ to throw the front door open and duck inside. With one last glance over her shoulder to make sure no one was watching, Kalina eased the door shut.

"Up to the third floor," she instructed.

It was a clumsy affair dragging the dummy up the two flights to the study but they managed it.

"This is a nice house," AJ said as they stopped outside the study so he could work a kink out of his wrist.

"Yeah. I spent a lot of time here when I was your age."

AJ wrinkled his nose. "Don't say it like that. It makes you sound old."

She swatted his arm. "I am old."

He rolled his eyes but resumed his grasp around the dummy's torso so they could maneuver it into the room. The window had been closed. Maybe Jimmy did it when he went back to collect the teacup.

"Put it against the chair," she said and went to unlatch the window.

"Man this place is kind of a mess," AJ responded.

"I'm sure people would say the same thing about your room." She turned back to face him. "So ... what's next?"

He retrieved his phone and fiddled with it for a minute. "Ok, so we just have to simulate someone being pushed, jumping or falling. Seems easy enough."

"Right. I think I should be the one to do the pushing. Nadine and I are about the same height and build. If I can get the dummy to land the right way then we will know if he was pushed."

"Got it. I'll head back downstairs."

She waited for him to reappear outside before she hefted the dummy over to the window. She turned it so that the dummy was facing her before she gave it a solid shove. It tipped over the windowsill and fell head over feet to the pavement below.

"Uh, Aunt K. I'm guessing the head is supposed to be over this dark spot," AJ called up.

Kalina leaned out the window to check the final position. The feet were where Mr. Larrabee's head should be and the dummy had landed face up. "Yeah. That clearly didn't work. Bring it back up."

AJ lugged the dummy back up the front porch and appeared in the hallway a few minutes later. She motioned for him to head back out and he groaned before doing as he was told. She waited until he was in position again and turned the dummy to face away from her before giving it a hard shove. It fell straight down but, again, wasn't in the right position.

"It's closer," AJ said.

"But not quite right. It's still too close to the house. Bring it up again."

He picked up the dummy roughly by one arm and started dragging it behind him. Kalina leaned farther out the window.

"Be careful with that!"

As she leaned back into the room, a thought occurred to her. If her theory were true then Nadine and Adam would be off the hook for Mr. Larrabee's death. AJ finally appeared and slumped into the office chair, not taking note of the blood specks on the leather. He set the dummy on the floor and wiped visible beads of sweat from his forehead.

"For a teenage boy you aren't in very good shape," Kalina scolded.

"I'm a nerd. Exercise is my kryptonite." He took several deep breaths before hoisting himself back to his feet. "I'll head back down."

"No, stick around up here. I think might have figured it out. And I think I need your help."

"What do you need me to do?"

"Help me lift the dummy so it's standing on the ledge."

"Seriously?"

"Just do it."

They lifted up the dummy and positioned it on the ledge of the window. Kalina looked at her nephew. "On the count of three, let go. One. Two. Three."

The both let go. Gravity took over and the dummy fell face first onto the pavement in the general spot where Mr. Larrabee had been discovered. AJ let out a low whistle.

"So he jumped."

"It certainly looks like it. I need to let Chris know."

"Remember, he's gonna be pissed at you."

Kalina smirked. "I'll make it up to him."

AJ gagged. "Gross. I didn't need to know that." He wandered over to the desk and started rifling through papers while Kalina pulled out her phone. "Hey, Aunt K. I think you should look at this."

"Don't touch it. It could be evidence."

He pulled his hands away and took a big step away from the desk. "Sorry."

"Just point to what you found," she said and walked over to stand beside him.

He indicated a pile of official looking documents with a notary seal at the bottom. She bent down to study the text more closely. "He was giving it back."

"Giving what back?"

She waved her nephew's question away. She walked to the other side of where he stood and nudged pages with the side of her phone. A handwritten page fluttered to the floor. She bent down to read it but didn't touch it.

"Oh, God."

AJ bent down to read it too and Kalina backed away, hitting 'Call' on her phone. It rang twice before someone answered.

"Ellesworth Police Department."

"Hi, I need to speak with Detective Harper right away."

There was a pause and then, "He's in an interrogation right now."

"I know. But I need to talk to him right away."

"Who should I say is calling?"

"Kalina. His girlfriend. It's about the case he's working. Please, just put him on the line."

She started to pace as the line went quiet. She could hear vague footsteps echoing on the other end of the line. Hopefully, her pleading had been enough to get the desk officer to summon Chris. Finally, the line clicked as someone picked up.

"Kal? What's going on?"

"I know what happened in Nadine's case."

"What are you talking about?"

"I know you're going to be angry with me but just hear me out. It would be better if you came to the Larrabees' house. Bring Nadine and Adam, too. They need to know what happened."

"We are definitely going to talk about this later." Chris's voice had taken on a hard edge of annoyance.

"Just get here, please."

12

Kalina and AJ waited on the front porch for everyone to arrive. AJ had turned pale after reading the note from Mr. Larrabee. She could understand his anxiety. It broke her heart a little to think that Mr. Larrabee had taken his own life. She only hoped it would somehow bring Nadine some comfort knowing that she hadn't blacked out and killed her father. Tires squealed in the distance and the squad car rolled up moments later. Chris climbed out, his face clouded with emotion. Nadine and Adam climbed out of the back. Neither said a word. Nadine was visibly shaking at the sight of her family home. Adam tried to place a hand on her shoulder but she shrugged it off. Kalina wondered what else had been revealed during that interview after she'd left.

"Why is there a CPR dummy in the driveway?" Adam asked.

"We were testing a theory," Kalina answered.

"What theory?" Nadine's voice was barely above a whisper.

"We were trying to figure out how your father landed the way he did. Whether he was pushed or fell."

"And?"

"He jumped. It looks like he climbed onto the windowsill and just let gravity take him."

Nadine's eyes welled with tears and she didn't try to stop them. They stained her cheeks in seconds. "Why would he do that?"

"It's better if you see what else we found."

"And what exactly did you find?" Chris kept his shoulders back and gaze straight ahead. All business.

"It's better if you see it for yourselves."

Chris briefly returned to the car to grab an evidence bag and some gloves before they all headed up to the study in a silent, single-file line. Kalina had made sure AJ hadn't moved the note from where it had landed on the floor. She would let Chris handle that. Immediately, Chris spotted the note and snapped on his gloves. After taking a cursory look he faced Kalina.

"Neither of you touched this?"

"No. I mean it fell when I was moving some other papers but I used my phone. We didn't touch anything."

"What is that?" Nadine asked.

Chris slid the note into the evidence bag and handed it over. "A suicide note."

Nadine's hands trembled as she took the

bag and sunk into the leather chair in the middle of the room.

Nadine,

I have spent so much time being angry about your mother's passing when I realize now it was my fault. I let my desire of material things get in the way of loving my only daughter and for that I am sorry.

The horrors I put you through are not something I can ever atone for. I do not seek your forgiveness. I only hope you are able to move forward with your life and be happy. Don't let the troubles of the past haunt you anymore.

Please don't see this as your fault. I have been struggling with this decision for some time. It is the only out I can see. I am truly sorry for everything.

Dad

The note fell to the floor as Nadine crumbled. A loud wail escaped her and filled the room. Adam picked up the fallen evidence and handed it back to Chris. Kalina went to wrap Nadine in a comforting hug, all the while wondering why Adam didn't seem surprised by the discovery.

"I missed something," Kalina said.

Chris tucked the evidence bag under his arm and blew out a breath. His shoulders relaxed a little. He was relenting. "Adam was here the night Mr. Larrabee killed himself." He looked to Adam. "You might as well explain."

Adam cleared his throat. "I was worried about Nadine. I came back to get her but, when I got here, she was out cold, or at least I thought she was. I came up here to confront Edwin about drugging his daughter again and I found him standing on the chair with a rope around his neck. I managed to get him down and... I tied him to the chair. I know it was stupid. I should have called the police but, to be honest, I was just in shock and a bit of a panic. I tied him up and I left. I knew it would look bad but at least he would be alive."

"So he was definitely alive when you left?" AJ interjected.

"Yes. He was. I didn't realize Nadine had woken up and untied him."

"I... I let him go so he could jump," she sobbed into Kalina's shoulder.

"It isn't your fault. None of it. He was sick for a while and he thought this was the only way he could make things right," Kalina whispered.

"He didn't have to kill himself."

"Grief makes people do unthinkable things," Chris said.

"That's a long time to hold on to grief," Kalina said.

"So, this is over then? The investigation is done? We aren't suspects anymore?" Nadine had stopped crying.

Chris's phone beeped, putting a halt to the conversation. He scrolled through whatever message he'd received. "The lab just came back with results on the rope we found as well as the tea. There were traces of both of your DNA on the rope along with Mr. Larrabee's. There were traces of NyQuil in the tea. So it sounds like you were drugged and the rest of the evidence lines up with the version of events you've shared. So, yes, it's over."

"There's one more thing"—Kalina pointed to the desk—"it looks like he changed his will."

Chris—still wearing gloves—picked up the paper from the top of the pile. "You're right. It looks like he deeded the house back to Nadine."

"After everything he went through to get the damn place and now he just gives it back?" Bitterness colored every word.

Adam bent down in front of her and took both of her hands in his. She didn't pull away this time. Apparently, knowing neither of them had been directly responsible was enough to thaw her emotions towards him. "You don't have to worry about it now. I think, as long as Detective Harper says it's okay, we should go back to the motel to get our stuff and leave town for a little while. We should put some distance between us and this place."

"Tomorrow. I just want to sleep. I haven't had a good night's sleep in a long time."

Adam pulled Nadine to her feet and with an affirmative nod from Chris they headed downstairs, no doubt in for a long walk back to the motel. Kalina looked at AJ and nodded her head towards the hallway but her nephew seemed oblivious to the hint.

"AJ, can you wait for me outside, please? Get the dummy back in the car, too."

He mouthed 'Good luck' on his way out, leaving Kalina and Chris alone. He set the evidence bag down on top of the will and crossed his arms over his chest.

"Go ahead and yell at me. I deserve it."

"You are too nosy for your own good

sometimes. We would have solved the case eventually but what you did helped."

Kalina stared, open-mouthed. "That's it? No rant about getting involved in police business or threatening the chain of evidence?"

"You didn't threaten the chain of evidence. You're smart enough not to touch things you aren't supposed to. Technically, this wasn't a crime scene anymore so you being here wasn't disturbing anything and thanks to you I got information out of Nadine sooner than I would have if you hadn't been around. I have a feeling Adam would have ended up stonewalling me in an effort to protect her. Hell, he might have even taken the fall for her if it came to that."

Kalina thought about mentioning Jimmy's role in her snooping but decided it wouldn't be very nice to throw the poor kid under the bus with Chris. She liked to think maybe she was giving Jimmy some on-the-job training in critical thinking along the way.

"You know what we need to get our minds off of this?" she said.

He shook his head. "No. What?"

"A game of Cards against Humanity. I've got a deck at home," she said with a smirk. After all, she'd told AJ she would find a way to make things up to Chris.

13

The next morning, Kalina rolled over in bed to find the space where Chris had been empty, the body heat dwindling. She sat up and rubbed at her eyes with one hand, searching for her phone with the other. After groping along the edge of her nightstand, she finally found her phone and checked the time: 7:02. She kicked the sheets aside and staggered out of the room. She found Chris standing by the coffee maker with two cups in hand.

"Hey, I didn't want to wake you," he said and handed her a mug.

"That's okay. I was planning on going for a run this morning anyway."

He spooned several generous helpings of sugar into his own mug and stirred before taking a sip. "Do you think you're going to stay in touch with Nadine?"

Kalina slid into a chair by the kitchen table and tugged at her hair. "Yeah. This whole time I felt like such a terrible friend. If I hadn't gone off to the city and been so lost in my own world and drama things might have been different."

"What do you mean? You couldn't have stopped any of this."

"Maybe not. But she wouldn't have felt so alone after her mother died. Maybe I would have noticed a change when her father was drugging her and could have gotten her help."

"Don't think about it like that. You were there for her now. As I said yesterday, you probably helped her keep it together through everything."

"I still can't believe you aren't mad at me for getting involved."

"Annoyed maybe but not mad."

"I swear I don't mean to get dragged into things. But I get curious and then I have to know what happened."

"I know. And it's why I love you. You are so concerned with the people of this town."

Kalina took another swig of coffee and laughed. "I was telling Nadine the other day that I was really glad to move back home because I didn't realize how much I missed the people. This is where I belong."

"Are you sure you want to go for a run? I could just drop you off at the shop on my way to the station."

"That's all right. I think I need the time to myself."

Chris downed the rest of his coffee in two big gulps and set the mug in the sink. He kissed her forehead before he disappeared to get dressed. She waited until he left before she went back to her room to pull on her workout clothes. Barring any unforeseen disasters, she fully intended to come home and shower before heading into work.

With ear buds in her ears, she took off at a steady jog. The weather was far more cooperative than it had been a few days ago and she settled into a comfortable rhythm. She took a different route, going up past the high school and fire department. She waved to a few of the firefighters heading on to their shifts as she went by. Veering off to the right at the next intersection, she found herself once again running along Ocean Front Drive. She hadn't intended go there but her subconscious must have been driving her. She stopped when she spotted a car in the driveway at 1609. She tugged the headphones out of her ears and approached it. The sound of running water caught her attention.

"Hello?" she called.

Water snaked down around the car's tires and she stepped out of its path. Kalina rounded the front of the car to find Adam holding a hose, washing away the last remnants of what had happened.

"Oh, hi," she said.

He shut off the water and tossed the hose aside. "Hi. If you're looking for Nadine, she's in the kitchen."

"Thanks."

She hadn't been looking for her friend but maybe they did need to talk. She wanted Nadine to know that she wanted them to remain close. Wiping her feet on the front mat, she headed straight back to the kitchen. Nadine sat at the table, staring at nothing in particular.

"Hey, I hope it's okay that I stopped by," Kalina said, snapping Nadine out of her fog.

"Yeah, of course."

Kalina took the seat across from her

friend. "I'm a little surprised you're back here. I thought you and Adam were heading out of town today."

"We will but we needed to get this place cleaned up. I wanted to take a few pictures of my mom, too."

"What are you going to do with it now that it's yours again?"

"Sell it. There is too much sorrow and sadness in this place for me to stay here. I don't need the reminder of all the horrible things I suffered because of these four walls. It tore our family apart and if I'm going to move forward and heal from this, I need to not be here. I need to make a clean break."

"That's understandable. I'm sure you'll find a buyer quick."

"Honestly, I don't even care about the money. I'll list it for whatever it's worth and take whatever I can get. I already called a broker, Thomas Chase. He's coming over this afternoon to do an appraisal."

"That is pretty quick."

"Like I said, I need a clean break." She twisted a few strands of hair together and looked down at her lap. "I have to write an obituary for my father. But I don't think I can do it yet. Adam said he talked to the coroner out in Salem and they are ready to release my father's body."

"You have time. And you don't have to do it alone. Adam and I are here for you."

"I just don't want people to ask questions. Knowing he took his life out of guilt is hard enough for me to deal with. I don't think I could handle everyone else knowing because then they would wonder what he felt guilty about. They'd assume it was my mother."

"You don't have to write that he took his life. You can say that he passed away suddenly while you were home visiting him. Keep it really vague. No one has to know the truth. It's your life and your family. You're in control of what happens now."

"What about a funeral? I can't pay for that. I don't even know if he wanted one. And I don't know what to do with his body. My mother was cremated but I have no idea if that's what he wanted, too. And do I put him with her or with his own family?"

"Have you looked at his will?"

"Adam did. I couldn't bring myself to look this morning."

"Then let him help you figure all of that out. That's what boyfriends are for, especially ones who are lawyers. He'll know what to do or he'll know the person to talk to. Lean on the people who care about you, Nadine."

"Thanks. It's just so overwhelming and I just want it to be over." Tears shone in her eyes but they didn't fall.

Kalina reached across the table to give her friend's hand a firm, reassuring squeeze. She looked around the kitchen at the familiar, pale yellow wallpaper and cream colored drapes. A tiny part of her would be sad to see it come into new ownership but she understood Nadine's desire to move on. It had been a harrowing few days for both of them but somehow they'd made it through. Maybe it was because they'd had each other for support.

"The reason I stopped by was because I wanted you to know that I don't want us to lose touch again, even if you're moving somewhere else with Adam."

"I'm glad you said that. I think it will be easier now. Besides, I know where to find you, Ms. Business Owner."

Kalina smiled. "It is pretty amazing that I actually got to become what I'd dreamed of and run the very store I'd always wanted."

"Not everyone is so lucky," Nadine said with a note of sadness in her voice.

"Things are going to work out for you. You've got a great guy in your life and you can put all of this behind you. We're still young. You have plenty of time to find what makes you happy. And if a nerdy mood strikes, you get the friends and family discount."

Nadine laughed a deep belly laugh. Her eyes crinkled at the corners and it had to be the happiest she'd been in a long time. It warmed Kalina's heart to see that, even with just kind words, she was helping her friend piece her life back together. Sure, tragedy had struck this family but the town was still at peace and unscathed.

When a debt collector goes missing on Thanksgiving, can Kalina keep her sleuthing nose clean? Or will the lure of another case be too much.
Grab Debts and Debtors to decipher the clues today.

GET FREE CONTENT

Sign up for my newsletter by clicking here to be kept up-to-date with my latest releases and receive your copy of Toil and Trouble as a free gift.

All Hallow's Eve brings dangerous secrets. Can Kalina get to the bottom of the mystery?

Subscribe and find out now!

ABOUT THE AUTHOR

S.E. Biglow is the pen name of *USA Today* bestselling author Sarah Biglow. She lives in Massachusetts with her husband and son. She is a licensed attorney and spends her days combatting employment discrimination as an

Investigator with the Massachusetts Commission Against Discrimination.

You can find an up-to-date list of all my books here

www.ingramcontent.com/pod-product-compliance
Lightning Source LLC
Chambersburg PA
CBHW031026190726
48286CB00003BA/1034